T0134798

A Journey To
Magic World

The Magical Orange Balloon

CHARISE KATZ

ILLUSTRATIONS DONE BY
ADYNA FERRE

Copyright © 2019 Charise Katz.

All rights reserved. No part of this book may be used or reproduced by any means, graphic, electronic, or mechanical, including photocopying, recording, taping or by any information storage retrieval system without the written permission of the author except in the case of brief quotations embodied in critical articles and reviews.

Balboa Press books may be ordered through booksellers or by contacting:

Balboa Press
A Division of Hay House
1663 Liberty Drive
Bloomington, IN 47403
www.balboapress.com.au
1 (877) 407-4847

Because of the dynamic nature of the Internet, any web addresses or links contained in this book may have changed since publication and may no longer be valid. The views expressed in this work are solely those of the author and do not necessarily reflect the views of the publisher, and the publisher hereby disclaims any responsibility for them.

Any people depicted in stock imagery provided by Getty Images are models, and such images are being used for illustrative purposes only.
Certain stock imagery © Getty Images.

Illustrator- Adyna Ferre
Cover of book- done by Balboa

ISBN: 978-1-5043-1829-7 (sc)
ISBN: 978-1-5043-1868-6 (e)

Print information available on the last page.

Balboa Press rev. date: 07/19/2019

BALBOA®
PRESS
A DIVISION OF HAY HOUSE

To all Kids Magic Life young adult students old, new and in between.

I thank you for bringing magic world to life and sharing in the dream, for your time and dedication to the live shows. I hope that each of you will take a little piece of magic world with you to keep in your heart, so that you might create your own magic world for your future.

You are the future generation that need to teach the little ones how to feel safe and loved and remember that we are all magical inside.

I have learnt from each of you, and you have given me a precious gift to remember that being young is wonderful and fun. May all your dreams come true.

Lots of love for your future journey Charise

The day is beautiful and the children are playing outside, under the big green tree drawing pictures in the sky with their finger.

"I can see a pirate!" says Tom.

I can see a mermaid!" says Lilly.

They giggle out loud, and sing joyfully

Tom, are you ready to go on another magical adventure?"

"Yes Lilly, but how do we call the Little Green Man?"

"We have to use our imagination, remember Tom, then he will come to us."

"Yes Lilly, I remember."

"Do you have the small orange balloon that he gave you?"

"Yes Lilly, here it is in my pocket."

"Well let's see if it works.

The children stand together under the big green tree holding the small orange balloon in their hands. They are so excited, and picture the Little Green Man inside the balloon and say the magic words.

"Life is a miracle

Life is a dream

There's magic inside me

Magic I believe"

They both stand there waiting and waiting for the magic to happen. They are so excited and nervous at the same time.

After a while the children open their eyes and look at one another.

Lilly and Tom giggle. "Well I don't know why, but we should be in magic world by now Lilly. That's what happened last time," says Tom.

"Let's do it again," says Lilly.

The children are just about to close their eyes again, when suddenly out of nowhere Lilly sees a large orange air balloon coming out of the sky heading towards them.

"Look Tom it's the Magical Orange Balloon!"

"Oh my gosh Lilly, you are right, and I can see the Little Green Man inside and he's waving to us."

Sure enough waving and shouting to the children was the Little Green Man.

"Top of the world to ya.

Top of the world to ya all, my friends."

As the balloon gets closer and closer to the ground it begins to slow down, until it is gently floating toward the big green tree and towards the children.

When the balloon lands on the ground, the Little Green Man steps out and walks up to the children and gives them a big hug.

"Well hello children," says the Little Green Man, and begins his song and dance.

"Let me introduce myself to you, I come out when the sky is very blue

When the children are laughing, and the love is true, and we don't have a care to do.

My name is Little Green man I say, I come to watch the children as they play, my heart is filled with love all day, and we don't have a care to say"…………..

"Top of the world to ya, and what a beautiful day it is to go on a magical adventure."

"Hello Little Green Man, it's so wonderful to see you again, says Lilly."

"Hello Tom how are you my boy?"

"I'm good thanks, Little Green man."

"Well children do you believe in magic yet?" asks the Little Green man?

"Yes, oh yes!" replies Lilly, waving her hands up in the air with great excitement.

"I do too!" replies Tom.

"Well, come along then children, step inside the Magical Orange Balloon and we will go on a magical journey!"

The Little Green man and the children sing as they walk towards the Magical Orange Balloon and climb inside.

"A magnificent orange, orange balloon. I can't wait to climb inside

Oh what a magical ride………………"

Gently floating above the clouds, higher and higher into the big blue sky, goes The Magical Orange Balloon.

The children giggle and laugh. "This is such fun!" shouts Lilly. "Look we're flying with the birds."

"I can touch the clouds," says Tom.

"Well children are we ready to say the magic words?" asks the Little Green Man.

"Life is a miracle

Life is a dream

There's magic inside me

Magic I believe"

The children, so excited, repeat the words very loudly.

When they look up they find themselves in a beautiful magical world.

There's no sign of the big green tree, just the most magnificent world you could ever imagine!

We're back in Magic World," says Lilly. "Look at all those beautiful, colourful rainbows and everything smells so sweet."

"Yes," says Tom, "we are definitely in Magic World. Listen to that wonderful music."

"Welcome to Magic World my friends," says The Little Green Man.

"Where are we going today?" asks Tom.

"Well I thought I might take you to meet some friends of mine this time," replies the Little Green Man.

"What are their names?" asks Lilly.

"Well, my first friend is Miss Jessie Bunny," says the Little Green Man.

"A Bunny rabbit?" asks Tom.

"Yes that's quite right Tom," says the Little Green Man.

"What is so special about a bunny rabbit? We have lots of them at home."

"Well, Tom this might come as a small surprise, but Miss Jessie is no ordinary bunny rabbit."

"How so?" asks Lilly.

"Ah my friends, you'll have to wait and see.

The balloon gets closer and closer to the ground and in the near distance the children can see a marvelous little red cottage nestled between the trees. The trees are long and steady, coming together like a beautiful dark green archway.

It looks so heavenly, the children sigh. "It's so beautiful here in Magic World, I wish I could live here forever!" says Lilly.

"Yes everything seems so peaceful," says Tom.

The Magical orange balloon comes to a stop and the group of friends step out onto a sandy beach. "I like the feeling of the sand between my toes," says Lilly, taking off her other shoe. "It feels so soft."

The Little Green man takes the lead and walks towards the archway of trees. "The trees invited you in like a friendly hand pointing the direction to the cottage.

As soon as they enter the archway they find a pebble stone pathway that leads them directly to the little cottage.

The cottage is so beautiful and is painted red with white awnings.

Next to the house is a little wooden bench with beautiful purple flowers painted on it.

Big beautiful colourful birds perching on either side of the cottage door nod to the children as they come closer.

There are flowers everywhere in all different colours, and a line of red rose bushes lead straight to the front door.

On the door is a message written in gold writing and it says, 'Please be quiet the flowers are resting.'

"Oh, what a happy place," Lilly beams.

"It's so peaceful," says Tom.

"Yes children this is Miss Jessie's House. She should be home soon.

We might have to wait a short while for her to get back."

"That's okay," says Lilly, "I want to take my time to smell the roses. They're so pretty."

Lilly sings.

"The smell of roses makes me feel so good, the smell of roses, all round the neighbourhood."…………..

Red and white roses fence in the darling little house.

Whilst the children are admiring the house, they suddenly hear singing coming down the pebble stone pathway and it seems to be a bunny rabbit holding a basket of flowers.

"I'm Jessie bunny so happy and free, I love the world and the world loves me.".............

Miss Jessie takes the long stemmed flowers out of her basket to smell them.

"Oh how beautiful these will look on my tea table," says Miss Jessie bunny.

When Miss Jessie looks up she sees the Little Green Man and the children.

"Hello, Little Green Man, how lovely to see you, and these must be the children you've told me so much about. Hello children, I am looking so forward to having our tea together."

The children, quite speechless by now, realise that they are witnessing a talking rabbit, dressed in a pretty blue and white polka dot dress, with red dance shoes.

"How strange!" says Tom.

"Yes it truly is," says Lilly.

"What is strange my dears?" asks Miss Jessie.

"Well you seem to be a talking, dancing rabbit and this is quite remarkable," says Tom.

"Oh, that my dears. Well let me tell you if you think I am strange wait until you meet

Mr. Floppy. Now there's a fella with a swing in his step."

As the children, the Little Green Man, and Miss Jessie sit down to tea, they hear a faint tapping sound in the distance, which seemed to be getting louder and closer.

When they look up, suddenly they see a tap dancing, singing bunny rabbit coming down the pebble stone pathway towards them.

"I'm Mr Floppy so happy and free, I'm a singing, dancing rabbit, that's me."..............

"I do believe that's Mr Floppy," says Miss Jessie bunny.

"Hello Mr Floppy, I've been waiting for you, and the children have been waiting too."

"Oh how wonderful! Hello children, hello Little Green Man, thank you for coming to Magic World to visit us."

The group hug, laugh and sit down to tea. Lilly and Tom have tea with the rabbits and the Little Green man.

"This is the most fun I have ever had," says Lilly.

"Yes, who would believe that we are having tea with talking rabbits and a Little Green man!" says Tom.

"Yes, this is truly wonderful. Please try my apple pie. It's my own home baked recipe," says Miss Jessie.

Mr. Floppy bursts into song.

"Miss Jessie's apple pie,

I'm certainly the guy, the luckiest by far,

it's candy apple sweet and boy it's a treat,

Miss Jessie's apple pie, so neat."

After tea the Little Green Man stands up and says.

"Well that was a splendid tea, Miss Jessie. Thank you."

"You are very welcome," says Miss Jessie with delight.

"Well children," says Mr. Floppy, "would you like to see some cool dance moves? After all I am a singing, dancing bunny rabbit who can tap dance like the wind."

"Oh yes, Mr Floppy we would love to see some of your cool dance moves," says Lilly with excitement.

"Well come along then children."

The children get up from the table and go to where Mr Floppy is standing

Mr Floppy hands the children a pair of tap shoes; a red pair for Lilly and a blue pair for Tom.

"Wow, my own tap shoes! I can learn how to tap dance now," exclaims Lilly.

"These are cool," says Tom, tip-tapping around the room.

"This is the most fun I have ever had!" says Lilly.

"Very good, now follow me," says Mr Floppy.

"We're tip-tapping to the sound of the beat

We're tip-tapping to the rhythm with our feet

We're tip-tapping on the cottage floor

We're tip-tapping cause we want some more

The children laugh and repeat the words.

Miss Jessie and the Little Green man come to join in with the singing.

Miss Jessie does a ballet dance and the little green man joins in with the tap dancing.

Then Miss Jessie and Mr Floppy dance together, filling the room with so much joy and love that you can feel the tingling in your feet.

After such a wonderful day, the Little Green man says, "I better get these children home."

"It's been a wonderful day Miss Jessie. I know the children have loved meeting you and Mr Floppy."

The group of friends walk out the door of the little house and back down the pebble stone pathway towards the Magical Orange Balloon.

"Wow that was great! Thank you Little Green Man," says Lilly.

"I'm glad you had such a good time, Lilly."

"Thank you for everything," says Tom.

The group give each other a great big hug and say goodbye.

"See you soon children," says Mr Floppy and Miss Jessie, waving goodbye.

"See you soon," shout the children as they step inside the Magical Orange Balloon with the Little Green man.

Soon they are flying gently in the air, once again.

Lilly and Tom start to fall asleep inside the Magical Orange Balloon. It has been a long adventure and they are both feeling very tired.

The Little Green Man sings the children a sleepy lullaby song.

"It's time to close our eyes, it's time to fall asleep

We stretch, we yawn, we say goodnight

It's been a busy week.

Just as the children are closing their eyes, the Little Green man says the magic words and get's the children to repeat them.

"Thank you for fulfilling all my good wishes."

When they open their eyes they find themselves lying back under the big green tree again.

The Little Green man has disappeared, and there is no sign of the Magical Orange Balloon.

Lilly opens her hand and finds a piece of paper with a note.

"Look Tom, it's a note from The Little Green Man and Miss Jessie Bunny."

"What does it say Lilly?"

Lilly opens up the piece of paper and reads the note out loud.

It says.............

Keep using those imaginations to make all your happy wishes come true, and remember your imagination is so powerful it can do whatever you want it too.

Love, the Little Green Man.

Hello my dears, this is a special drawing for you. A Magical Candy Floss dream house just waiting for you. So close your eyes and imagine what fun it will be, with Mr Floppy and I and the Little Green man makes three. We'll travel with you in the Magical Orange Balloon; I can't wait for our next adventure. I know it will be soon.

Love, Miss Jessie Bunny.

"Oh wow, Lilly, I can't wait for our next adventure," says Tom.

"Me too," says Lilly. "Oh what fun it will be. Now what do you think we have to do with this picture of a house?"

"It's called the Magical Candy Floss Dream House," says Tom.

"Why do you suppose it's called that Tom?" asks Lilly.

"Maybe we have to imagine a house covered in sweet pink candy floss Lilly," says Tom.

"I can do that Tom. I'm doing it right now and I can imagine travelling with Mr Floppy, Miss Jessie bunny and the Little Green Man in the Magical Orange Balloon to visit the Magical Candy Floss Dream House."

"That does sound like an interesting adventure and it would be very strange to visit a house made of candy floss. Then again, who would believe that we had tea with talking rabbits and a Little Green Man, and travelled to a place called Magic World in a Magical Orange Balloon!" says Tom.

"Yes," giggles Lilly, "who would believe such a story?"

Well, we will have to wait and see. Join us again under the big green tree and we'll travel to Magic World just you and me.

The end.

Printed in the United States
By Bookmasters